"Hello, Mister."

Leroy bowed low. "Just call me Leroy, Jolene. That'll suit me fine."

I didn't want to call him anything. "Hello, Mister," I said. It seemed like the best thing to say. If I called him Leroy, he might think he had a chance of being special to me.

Momma didn't hear me call him Mister, but Grandpa did. He frowned, lowering his thick gray eyebrows. I was afraid Grandpa was about to order me to apologize.

Leroy tilted his head back and laughed so loud I thought the walls would tumble down. His whole body shook, and he slapped his hat against his knee. "Jolene, I've been called a lot of things in my life, but I ain't never heard nobody call me plain Mister."

OTHER PUFFIN CHAPTERS
YOU MAY ENJOY

MISTER
AND ME

KIMBERLY WILLIS HOLT

WITH ILLUSTRATIONS BY
LEONARD JENKINS

PUFFIN BOOKS

My heartfelt thanks go out to each of the following people:

Louise Guillory, Beatrice Triplett, Emma Moore, and Andrew Napoleon for telling me about living and working in a sawmill town. Verda Ruff, Troy DeRamus, and Janet Tompkins of the Louisiana Forestry Association for helping with the details. Ivon Cecil, Chery Webster, Pat Willis, Carol Winn, Jennifer Archer, and Robin Quackenbush for their honest feedback. My agent, Jennifer Flannery, for believing in my work, and my editor, Kathryn Dawson, for her insight and direction.

And a special thanks to my dad, Ray Willis, who first told me about Long Leaf.

PUFFIN BOOKS
Published by the Penguin Group
Penguin Putnam Books for Young Readers,
345 Hudson Street, New York, New York 10014, U.S.A.
Penguin Books Ltd, 27 Wrights Lane, London W8 5TZ, England
Penguin Books Australia Ltd, Ringwood, Victoria, Australia
Penguin Books Canada Ltd, 10 Alcorn Avenue, Toronto, Ontario, Canada M4V 3B2
Penguin Books (N.Z.) Ltd, 182-190 Wairau Road, Auckland 10, New Zealand

Penguin Books Ltd, Registered Offices: Harmondsworth, Middlesex, England

First published in the United States of America by G. P. Putnam's Sons,
a division of Penguin Putnam Books for Young Readers, 1998
Published by Puffin Books,
a division of Penguin Putnam Books for Young Readers, 2000

13 15 17 19 20 18 16 14 12

Text copyright © Kimberly Willis Holt, 1998
Illustrations copyright © Leonard Jenkins, 1998
All rights reserved

THE LIBRARY OF CONGRESS HAS CATALOGED THE G. P. PUTNAM'S SONS EDITION AS FOLLOWS:
Holt, Kimberly Willis. Mister and me / Kimberly Willis Holt;
with illustrations by Leonard Jenkins. p. cm.
Summary: In a small Louisiana mill town in 1940, Jolene does not want her
Momma to marry the logger who is courting her, but it seems that even
her most defiantly bad behavior cannot make him go away.
[1. Remarriage—Fiction. 2. Family life—Louisiana—Fiction.
3. Afro-Americans—Fiction. 4. Lumbermen—Fiction. 5. Louisiana—Fiction.]
I. Jenkins, Leonard, ill. II. Title. PZ7.H745Mi 1998 [Fic]—dc21 97-40329 CIP AC
ISBN 0-399-23215-X

Puffin Books ISBN 0-698-11869-3

Printed in the United States of America

CHAPTER 1

Momma's sewing machine clanked all week long. Sometimes I woke up and heard the Singer before the morning sawmill whistle blew. And sometimes I fell asleep at night listening to the rhythm of the foot pedal hitting the floor. But tonight was Friday and we were going to the picture show. So Momma tucked the machine away in a corner like a broom waiting to be used again.

As we waited for Florence's family to pick us up, I folded my arms across my chest, trying to look innocent. But it was too late.

Momma's hands flew to her hips. "Jolene Jasmine Johnson, what are you hiding under your coat?"

I unbuttoned my coat and pulled out the wooden frame. Daddy smiled up at me from the picture.

Momma's face softened and she knelt next to me. "Oh, Jolene. Why are you taking your daddy's picture to the show? It's the only one we have of him."

I stared at the hole in the floor that Grandpa had patched with pages from the *Saturday Evening Post*. I couldn't tell Momma I wanted to take Daddy's picture because I couldn't take him. If Florence could bring her daddy to the movies every Friday night, I wanted to bring mine, too.

Momma reached out and pulled me close to her. "It's hard not having a daddy. You were such a little thing when he died. He loved you, Jolene. He loved you more than anyone."

"More than you?" I asked.

She laughed. Red lipstick covered her lips. Red as her name—Ruby. "Well, a man loves a wife in a different way. I guess he loved us the same amount."

Then I asked her what I always asked, even though I knew the answer. "More love than could fill the state of Louisiana?"

Momma always answered, "More love than could fill every state in the United States—all forty-eight." But today she looked away kind of sad and said, "More love than could fill this great big world."

Momma gently took the picture from me. She put

it next to the Emerson radio that she bought last summer with money earned sewing dresses for the white women who lived in the mill town.

Then Grandpa limped in from his bedroom just as Abe, Florence's daddy, honked his truck's horn. Years ago, Grandpa had hurt his leg in a logging accident. Now he worked in the mill, sawing logs into lumber.

"Goodnight, Grandpa!" I said, running out the door.

"Save me some buttered popcorn," he hollered.

Momma said Grandpa didn't go to the picture show because he liked to have peace and quiet after hearing the saws run all day. He once told me that he cut so much lumber during the day that when he closed his eyes at night he could still see lumber and clouds of sawdust. "Can't a workin' man get no rest?" he'd say.

Momma slipped inside the pickup next to Florence's momma, Harriet, and I hopped in the back next to Florence. In the summer, I loved to ride in the back and feel the warm breeze hit my face. But it was January, and the cold air nipped my cheeks.

A million stars scattered across the dark sky and the giant pine trees formed a ruffled trim. I pointed to a group of stars. "Look. I bet that's the Big Dipper."

Ever since my teacher taught us that the stars made pictures in the sky called constellations, I liked to pretend the Big Dipper was Daddy watching over me. But I could never find it among the stars.

Florence peered up at the sky. She was covered with blue: a knitted blue hat on her head, a blue wool scarf wrapped around her neck, my old blue coat Momma made, and thick blue socks that went up to her knees. Momma said when Florence was born, she was so tiny she could fit in her daddy's hand. That's the reason, Momma said, that Florence caught a lot of colds, and the reason Harriet dressed her as if we lived in snow-covered mountains.

"What do you think will be playing at the picture show tonight?" I asked.

Florence shrugged her shoulders like she did every Friday night.

"Do you think it might be Hopalong Cassidy?" He was my favorite western movie star.

She just shrugged again.

"Florence, you never say anything. Has the cat got your tongue?"

Florence's eyes popped wide open. "When I got something to say, I'll say it."

Maybe Florence didn't get enough words dumped into her head since she was born so early. I had so many words and questions bouncing around inside me, I thought I'd never live long enough to say them all.

We drove past the company store, the barber shop, and the hotel where the single mill workers lived. We passed the post office, the meat market, the school for the white mill children, then our school. In Logan's mill town we had everything we needed—except picture shows.

A few minutes later we arrived in Glenmora. *"Happy New Year—1940"* signs were posted on every store window. Even though it was dark, I could see the pretty china doll with brown curls in Randall's general store window. I had hoped to get her for Christmas. I had even given her a name—Brenda Jane. When Christmas morning arrived and I didn't receive her, I had been disappointed. But Momma said maybe next year.

Abe parked along Main Street with the other cars and trucks. A marquee sign read *"South of the Border,* starring Gene Autry."* He was almost as good as Hopalong Cassidy.

We stood in the concession line for popcorn. I loved watching the kernels pop out of the cooker in fluffy white coats, and smelling their roasty scent.

Suddenly someone with a booming laugh entered the lobby. I turned and saw Leroy Redfield and some of the other men who worked for the sawmill. Grandpa had known Leroy for years. He was always telling us about something funny Leroy had said. But it always sounded stupid to me.

Leroy was a flathead. That's what folks called the

men who sawed down the pine trees and cut them into logs. Grandpa said they called loggers flatheads because if a tree fell on a logger's head, it would flatten it. Sometimes Florence and I played near the railroad tracks when the five o'clock train brought the flatheads back to the mill town. Leroy was the biggest, loudest, sweatiest flathead getting off the train.

When Leroy saw Momma in the picture show lobby, he stopped laughing and tipped his hat. "Howdy-do, Ruby."

Momma smiled shyly. "Well hello, Leroy."

The other men walked toward the stairs. "Come on, Leroy," one man said. "Let's get a seat."

Leroy just stood there looking at Momma, grinning. "Leroy," the man repeated.

"Umm, I'm right behind you." He tipped his hat again and said, "I hope you enjoy the show, Ruby."

"Thank you," Momma said. She watched Leroy walk up those stairs until he disappeared.

My stomach got a funny feeling in it, and I hadn't even taken one bite of popcorn yet.

After Momma paid for our popcorn, we climbed the stairs to the balcony with the other colored people. As always, the white folks sat downstairs. It didn't seem fair. "Why do we have to sit up here?" I asked.

"Hush, Jolene," Momma said, frowning.

Florence frowned, too, and shook her head at me like she was all grown up.

Soon the velvet curtains opened and Mr. Autry rode onto the screen with his horse, Champion. I forgot about having to sit upstairs. The next hour flew by like minutes.

As the music played at the end of the movie, I closed the top of the popcorn sack with a handful left inside for Grandpa. I hoped he wouldn't mind those kernels.

The only thing good about the movie being over was that we always bought an ice cream cone at the concession stand before leaving. My mouth watered as I stood in line between Momma and Florence, trying to decide if I wanted strawberry or vanilla.

Leroy stood behind Momma. When we got to the cashier, he took out some coins and offered to pay for our ice cream—like we didn't have any money.

I held my breath. Then Momma said, "No, thank you, Leroy. That wouldn't be right."

I felt better until we were leaving the picture show and Leroy winked at Momma and said, "See you soon, Ruby."

I could have gone the rest of my life and been happy if I never set eyes on Mr. Leroy Redfield again.

CHAPTER 2

The next Friday evening Momma changed into her yellow Sunday church dress. She also wore it to Wednesday night prayer meetings. But she never wore it to the picture show on Friday nights.

"Aren't we going to the picture show, Momma?"

She dabbed rose water on her wrists. "Grandpa will go with you tonight."

"Why aren't you coming? Do you have a special church meeting?"

"No, Jolene. Tonight, Mr. Leroy Redfield is taking me dancing."

Smiling, she touched my cheek with her cool hand. Her wrists smelled like a June day.

I didn't like thinking about my momma dancing with Mr. Leroy Redfield or about him smelling Momma's rose-scented wrists.

"But you don't dance," I said.

"I used to dance all the time, didn't I, Daddy?"

Grandpa sat in the chair by the old woodstove, his feet propped up on a foot stool. "She sure did, Jolene. Your momma kicked up her heels and shimmied with the best of them." He lowered his legs and tapped his toes on the floor.

"In fact," said Momma, "your grandpa taught me to shimmy."

"Show me how to shimmy, Momma," I begged. "Teach me to dance."

Momma turned up the radio. Count Basie's band was playing "One O'Clock Jump." Her shoulders shook to the beat of the music. I shook mine too. Then she grabbed my hands, twirling me around. The room started to spin. I felt as dizzy as the time I rode a Ferris wheel at the Louisiana State Fair.

She smiled wide, her straight white teeth gleaming, freshly brushed with tooth powder. I hoped when I grew up I would be as pretty as Momma.

I laughed as we whirled across the wood floor. Then Leroy knocked at the door, breaking our magic moment. At first, I saw two Leroys, until my head settled and my eyes focused.

"Well, Ruby-Gal," Leroy said, removing his hat, then holding it to his chest. "You look as pretty as moonlight."

Leroy was dark as a starless night, tall and thick as a long-leaf pine tree. He smelled good, too, but not like the rose water Momma wore. He smelled spicy like nutmeg in an apple pie. Tonight he wore creased pants instead of the logging overalls he wore to work every day.

"Wait a minute, Leroy," Momma said. "I need to get my purse. Jolene, where's your manners? Aren't you going to greet Mr. Redfield?"

Leroy bowed low. "Just call me Leroy, Jolene. That'll suit me fine."

I didn't want to call him anything. "Hello, Mister," I said. It seemed like the best thing to say. If I called him Leroy, he might think he had a chance of being special to me.

Momma didn't hear me call him Mister, but Grandpa did. He frowned, lowering his thick grey eyebrows. I was afraid Grandpa was about to order me to apologize.

Leroy tilted his head back and laughed so loud I thought the walls would tumble down. His whole body shook, and he slapped his hat against his knee. "Jolene, I've been called a lot of things in my life, but I ain't never heard nobody call me plain *Mister*."

He seemed to be waiting for me to smile, but I turned and scampered into the bedroom I shared with Momma. She stood in front of the mirror, smoothing her hair at the temples.

"Why do you have to go dancing with *him?*" I asked.

"Because, honey, I want to go dancing with Leroy."

"But *I* can dance now. Take *me* dancing."

She smiled and stroked my cheek. "One day, you'll grow up and a young man will take you dancing. I'm afraid that day will be here before I know it."

I shook my head back and forth and plopped on the edge of the bed. "Never! I'll never go dancing with anyone but you or Grandpa."

She chuckled and said, "We'll see." Turning her back to me, she asked, "Are my seams straight?"

The stocking seams ran down her leg as straight as a line drawn with a ruler. "Yes, ma'am," I said, wishing they were crooked.

I followed her into the front room. Leroy sat across from Grandpa. His huge body took up almost half the couch. Grandpa looked smaller than I had ever noticed, as if having Leroy in the room had caused him to shrink. Leroy stood when Momma entered the room. Then he helped her put on her coat.

"What time will you be home?" I asked.

Grandpa cleared his throat. He was sure to say

something to me this time, I thought, but Leroy spoke instead.

"Oh, I think I can get this young lady back home by, say . . . ten o'clock. Is that okay with you?" He guided Momma to the door, his hand under her elbow. "Goodnight, Foster, and goodnight to you, too, Jolene." He bowed before opening the door.

Momma kissed the top of my head, then she slipped out into the night with Leroy. "Have fun at the picture show."

Kneeling on the couch, I watched from the window as they left, wishing it was Momma and me. Not Leroy. He opened his truck door for her like she was a princess climbing into a coach. I hoped Leroy's good manners didn't fool her. Leroy's truck pulled away, rattling and huffing like it wanted someone to put it out of its misery.

Grandpa tapped me on the shoulder. "Enough, Jolene. Go get your coat on before Abe gets here."

"I don't feel so good," I said, holding my stomach. Maybe if Momma came home and found me sick in bed, she'd regret going dancing with Leroy.

Grandpa shook his head. "Well, I guess there's only one thing to do." Before I knew it, I had to swallow a spoonful of nasty tasting Squibb's cod-liver oil. Then Grandpa sent me to bed.

A moment later, I heard Abe's truck pull up and

honk. Grandpa hollered from the porch, "Jolene won't be going tonight. Have a good time." He didn't even tell them I was sick. Now Florence probably thought I was in trouble.

How could I sleep while Momma danced with Leroy? From bed, I watched the clock on our dresser. The little hand moved slowly, but finally arrived at the ten. I waited until the big hand touched the twelve. The moment it did, I tiptoed to the window and peeped through the flour-sack curtains.

Fifteen minutes later, the truck rattled to a stop in front of our house. My heart sprang from my chest. Momma and Leroy walked toward the porch, talking in hushed voices. Then Momma giggled at something Leroy said.

I dashed out of our bedroom and reached the front room just as Momma turned the knob and opened the door. When she saw me, she jumped.

"Jolene! What are you doing up?"

I placed my hands on my hips and stared at Leroy. "Mister," I said. *"You* are *late!"*

CHAPTER 3

The next day, Momma and I buttoned up our coats and headed toward the worn path behind the white folks' houses. A few dogs barked at us as we passed their yards.

Every house on our street looked exactly the same. All shotgun houses. If someone aimed a bullet through the front door, it would travel straight through to the back door.

Momma carried Miz Logan's new dress on a hanger, holding it high so the hem didn't drag on the ground. The dress looked as green as the pine needles I whiffed every time the wind blew. We took the shortcut on the trail through the woods. Momma held the tree limbs back so we wouldn't get scratched.

"What's Miz Logan want a green dress for?" I asked.

"I guess because she wants a green dress."

"She'll look like a Christmas tree with her red hair."

Momma stopped walking and whipped around, facing me. "Jolene Jasmine Johnson, watch your tongue, child."

"Yes ma'am."

Momma's eyes stayed fixed on me. "And you can't be sassy to Leroy, Jolene. I won't allow that kind of talk anymore." It was the first time she mentioned me meeting her and Leroy at the door the night before.

"But he's not my daddy." I barely remembered Daddy. He died from the fever when I was three. In that one picture we have of him, he is leaning against a tree. And *he* is handsome. Not ugly like Leroy. Not loud like Leroy, either. Grandpa said Daddy was a quiet man. The only thing I remember about my Daddy is that he whistled a lot.

"Leroy's an adult, Jolene, and due your respect. Understood?"

I swung the brown paper bag filled with leftover scraps from the green dress. "Yes ma'am."

Most of the women in the sawmill town let

Momma keep the scraps. Momma gave them to me and I saved them for the doll clothes I was going to sew for Brenda Jane. But Miz Logan wanted each tiny piece returned, like a mouse eating every crumb of bread dropped on the floor. She always bought the prettiest fabric in the whole town. Maybe in the entire state of Louisiana.

Mr. Logan owned the mill and everything else in town. The commissary, the cafe, the hotel where Leroy lived, and all the houses, too. The Logans lived on a hill above mill town in a huge white house with tall pillars in front of a wraparound porch.

Florence's momma, Harriet, worked as Miz Logan's housekeeper. When Harriet opened the door for us, her face broke into a grin. "Lawd, Ruby, not another dress. Don't you think I got enough laundry to do?" She winked at me.

Suddenly, we heard Miz Logan's high heels tapping on the floor. She had scarlet hair and a turkey neck like President Roosevelt's wife. "Why, Ruby, are you finished already? My, you're not only a wonderful seamstress, you're fast, too."

Momma had worked many late nights to finish the dress. She told me once, "The quicker I finish, the quicker I get paid." But now she shyly gazed at the floor and said, "Oh, Miz Logan, it ain't hard."

Miz Logan took the dress from Momma and carried it to the giant picture window, studying it in the sunlight. Her eyes scanned the dress from the collar to the hemline. For a long moment, she didn't say anything.

Momma bit her lower lip and kept her head down like she was praying.

I wanted to say, "You'll never find anything wrong with my momma's sewing. She was born with a needle in her hand." That's what Grandpa said. But then I remembered Momma's talk about my tongue. I didn't think she'd be happy if I said those words to a white woman. Even though they were true.

Finally, Miz Logan turned toward Momma and me. "Beautiful, as usual, Ruby. God has given you a great gift."

Momma's shoulders let down some, as if she had held her breath waiting for Miz Logan to say she liked the dress.

"Did you remember the scraps?" Miz Logan asked.

"Yes ma'am." Momma nudged me.

Stepping forward, I handed Miz Logan the brown paper sack.

"Thank you, Joann," Miz Logan said.

"It's Jolene," I snapped.

Momma pinched my arm. It didn't hurt, but it startled me.

"Ma'am," I added in a softer voice.

Why did Momma always act afraid of Miz Logan? Miz Logan didn't seem to notice what I said anyway. She walked to the oval dining room table and pulled something out of a bag. More fabric. Beautiful cornflower-blue fabric. When Miz Logan held it up for us to see, the chandelier light made it shine like no cloth I'd ever seen before. It didn't look like silk, and it sure wasn't cotton.

"Velvet!" The word floated out of Momma's mouth like a feather, drifting slowly down until it reached my ears.

Miz Logan paid Momma and gave her a picture to copy for the velvet dress. Her Valentine dress, she called it. The Logans planned to host a fancy party with a real band. They kept one room in their house just for dancing. Harriet had told us the Logans called it the ballroom. I'd have given anything to dance with Momma on a ballroom floor.

On the way home, I asked Momma, "Do you think Miz Logan will invite you and Harriet to the party?"

Momma shook her head. "No, of course not."

"Well, she said she was inviting everyone they know."

"That's not what she meant. She meant all the rich white people they know."

"Why didn't she say that, then? Why didn't she just say what she meant?"

"Everyone is not like you, Jolene. Not everyone says what comes through their head the moment it pops in there."

Before the last sawmill whistle blew, Momma spread the velvet out on our table. Grandpa would want to eat supper as soon as he came home from work, but it was as if Momma couldn't wait to unfold the fabric. Her hand stroked the velvet over and over. Her eyes combed every inch of that fabric. She made me want to touch it.

My hand reached toward the velvet, but Momma grabbed my wrist. She examined my palm. "Are your hands clean?"

"Yes ma'am. I washed them after I ate lunch."

"Okay, you can touch it, but not too much. You'll wear the sheen off."

I brushed my hand across the surface and giggled. Velvet tickled, but what a nice tickle. This must be what butterfly wings felt like.

"Miz Logan is gonna have the prettiest dress at the party, isn't she?"

"Maybe," Momma said. "If it were me, I would have picked red."

"You'd be beautiful in red, Momma, but can you imagine Miz Logan in red with *her* hair? She'd look like a dancing Valentine heart."

Momma's chuckle started off slow, then it worked itself up to a deep belly laugh. I joined her and didn't stop until Grandpa walked into the house with Leroy. Grandpa flopped down into his chair.

"What's so funny?" Leroy asked us, his hands tucked in his overall pockets.

I shrugged my shoulders and took the hot water bottle Momma had filled over to Grandpa. While I held it next to his crippled leg, I watched Momma and Leroy.

Momma was staring at her scissors. She shook her head and snapped her tongue against the roof of her mouth.

"What's wrong, Ruby-Gal?" Leroy moved up next to Momma until their shoulders touched. The hair on the back of my neck stood up.

"My scissors," Momma said. "They're too dull to cut this velvet. They haven't been sharpened since last year."

Leroy wrapped his arm around Momma. "No need to fret. I can sharpen them for you with my whetstone. If I can keep my pocket knife sharp, I can surely keep a little ol' pair of scissors sharp, too."

Momma's forehead wrinkled. "Will it be any trouble?"

"Ain't no trouble. After all, you're cooking my dinner."

I didn't know what I liked least. Leroy sharpening Momma's scissors, his staying for dinner, or the way his heavy arm circled Momma's bony shoulders.

CHAPTER 4

Sunday morning, folks poured into the church wearing their finest clothes. Even Florence tied new blue ribbons to her braids. Both men and women wore hats, but the men took their hats off before going inside. The ladies' hats looked like they had been dipped in a rainbow—lavender, pink, red, or yellow like Momma's.

Today we were having a church rally to raise money for a new roof. Churches from all over Rapides parish would come to our worship service and put money in the offering. In return, we would serve them dinner. Last summer, we had a rally for a piano and we ate outside on blankets spread over the grass.

But today, the January cold would keep our meal indoors.

Grandpa, Momma, and I stood on the church steps visiting with friends while the piano started playing "We're Marching to Zion."

Leroy came up the road swinging his arms, a Bible in one hand. I had seen enough of his face in the last two days.

He tipped his hat to Miz Hopkins and Miz Cook. They looked like grannies to me, but Grandpa called them old maids.

"Howdy-do," Leroy said. The old maids nodded and smiled.

I wished we could have hurried into the church before Leroy reached us. But he headed toward Momma like a wise man following the Star of Bethlehem.

"I'll get us a seat," Grandpa said. He entered through the open doors.

Momma waited in her yellow dress, smiling at Leroy while he grinned back. I could have been invisible.

He removed his hat and half bowed. "Ruby-Gal," he said. "It's a fine morning on our good Lord's day."

"Yes it is, Leroy. Yes it is."

I looked at the sky. Grey clouds hid the sun, and the crisp air chilled me to the bone.

"How are you, Miz Jolene?" Leroy asked.

I raised my nose in the air. "Fine, Mister."

"Jolene!" Momma said.

"Quite all right, Ruby-Gal. 'Mister' is kinda growing on me." He waited for Momma and me to step in front of him and lead the way to our pew.

Grandpa's arm stretched across the back of the space where Momma and I usually sat. But today, we had to make room for Leroy. Grandpa scooted over, and I slid in beside him. Momma settled next to me, and Leroy sat on the end. His heavy body made the old pew creak. I hoped he didn't break it, causing all of us to fall. The thought of us on the floor with our shoes dancing in the air made me giggle.

Momma glared at me and I bit my inner cheek. If the pew did break, maybe Momma would see a different picture of Leroy. Maybe then she'd think Leroy was a clumsy ox.

The choir entered from the back of the church. We stood, joining them in the song. "We're Marching to Zion" was my favorite hymn. I loved the part where we sang "beautiful, beautiful Zion."

At least I *usually* loved that part, but today Leroy was singing, too. And by the loud way he sang, the congregation must have thought he was trying out for the church choir. He had no shame. Just tossed his head back and let the words boom out in his deep bullfrog voice.

My face burned. Across the room, Florence hid her

grin behind her hand. I glanced up at Momma. She beamed at Leroy like his voice was the sweetest sound she had ever heard. He reminded me of an old black rooster sitting on our fence, proudly crowing away as if he cooed as pretty as a dove.

During the sermon, Leroy's arm rested on the back of the pew, leaning against Momma. When his fingers barely touched my neck, I cringed. Leroy moved his hand, then cupped it over Momma's shoulder.

Smells from baskets of fried chicken under the pews rose up around us. My mouth watered. Momma had baked two buttermilk pies. Her pies were the best in the mill town because she used an extra egg and more butter.

Later, in the serving line, Leroy piled two big slices of Momma's pie on his plate. I guess he thought he would impress Momma, but I hoped he would embarrass her. After all, other people liked buttermilk pie, too.

Just as we had filled our plates, rain began to hammer on the roof. Women scattered around the church, placing empty pots and bowls under the leaks to catch the raindrops. *Tink, tink, tink* could be heard all around us.

Everyone grabbed their plates and found a place to sit. Grandpa talked with some men in the choir section. I could see him rubbing his chin and shaking his head.

Momma and Leroy sat by themselves in the front pew. Every minute or so, Momma giggled like a little girl. I wondered what she thought was funny about Leroy besides his face.

Florence and I settled in a back pew, eating, as we watched Momma and Leroy. As usual, Florence stayed quiet. Momma said if I didn't talk so much Florence might say something every once in a while. That's why I was surprised when Florence opened her mouth and asked, "When do you reckon your momma and Mr. Leroy will get married?"

My fork clinked against my plate. I stared at Florence without blinking until she squirmed. Finally I said, "My momma isn't marrying anyone because she has Grandpa and me. And that's enough." But as I listened to Momma laugh with Leroy, I wondered if we *were* enough.

CHAPTER 5

After school Wednesday, Momma and I hurried to the company store to purchase more thread for Miz Logan's Valentine dress. Momma was particular about matching the fabric, so she took a scrap with us. Some customers bragged about her tiny stitches. Miz Logan called them *invisible*.

Grandpa said Momma should charge extra for thread. But Momma said, "If I charge for every little thing, the customers will be fussy about my sewing." She never even let me help her with the handwork, even though I knew how to sew doll clothes.

In the store, sweet candy scents mixed with strong smells from baskets of onions and garlic bulbs. Glass jars of penny candy lined the counter—vanilla taffy, sour lollipops, and my favorite, red-and-white striped peppermint sticks.

Momma headed to the back of the store, where dried goods were kept. The thread was next to the few bolts of fabric the store carried.

"Oh, look, Jolene," Momma said. "Red velvet." Her hand stroked the velvet back and forth the same way I petted Florence's cat, Reba. The red velvet was next to the bolt of blue. The two fabrics shined like jewels among the plain cottons.

I rubbed my hand across the fabric. Red velvet tickled just like the blue.

"Isn't it the finest thing you ever saw?" Momma asked.

Before I could speak, a voice boomed behind us. "Why, yes, ma'am, I do believe it is."

"Leroy!" Momma said. "What are you doing here?"

Yes, I thought, *what are you doing here?*

His hands hid in the pockets of his overalls. Today he didn't smell like nutmeg. He smelled like a sweaty flathead.

"The handle broke on the saw we were using, so my boss asked me to pick up another one." He squatted in front of me like I was a little kid, meeting me eye to eye. "How about a peppermint stick, Jolene? Or are you already sweet enough?"

My mouth watered at the word peppermint. It was a rare treat to have any kind of sweet. Sometimes Grandpa gave me a stick of Beech-Nut gum. But the last peppermint stick I had had came in my Christmas sock. I had planned to make the peppermint last a whole week, but I barely made it two days.

"No, thank you, Mister." I regretted those words as soon as I said them.

"Well, *I* sure want me a peppermint stick." He bought one, then broke it and held out half to me. "But I can't eat a whole peppermint. Can't you help me?"

This time, I accepted. "Thank you, Mister," I grumbled.

After paying for the thread, Momma and I headed home. Even though the sun still hung high in the sky, I could see a faded sliver of the moon. Pine needles crunched beneath our feet and saws whined in the distance. Momma was as quiet as a church on Monday morning. I sucked the sweet peppermint stick and wondered if her head was filled with thoughts of pretty red velvet or that stinky Leroy.

CHAPTER 6

February days were short. Before dinner, the sun began to set in purple clouds. One afternoon, Florence and I were picking up coal near the tracks when Leroy came walking toward us. I wondered why he wasn't still at work.

Leroy carried a sack in his hand like the ones they used at the company store. It could be filled to the rim with peppermint sticks for all I cared. This time I wasn't going to accept anything from Leroy, not even sweet-tasting candy.

Leroy towered above us, grinning like a possum. "Florence, would you mind if I talk to Jolene in private here a minute?"

I wanted to grab Florence by a pigtail and say, "Don't you move one inch." But before I could blink, she stood, brushed red dirt from her clothes, and said, "No sir. Don't mind at all." Off she ran, fast as ice cream melts on a summer day.

Leroy motioned to a huge stump. "Let's sit down right here."

He dusted off the stump with a handkerchief, plopped his big bottom down, and stretched out his long legs.

"Aaahh!" he said. "I'm so tired my bones ache." He glanced up at me. "Ain't you gonna sit down?"

I sat on the edge of the stump, more off than on. I didn't want Leroy to think sitting next to him was pleasant.

"The boss let me off early since I worked late for him yesterday."

"I gotta be getting back home," I said.

"This won't take but a minute," he said. "Looky there." He pointed across the tracks to a bare patch on the hill. "That's where we've been cutting timber. Pretty soon that hill will be as bare as my head."

Surely, he hadn't asked Florence to leave so he could show me where the flatheads had been logging and talk about his bald head.

The saws stopped their lonesome whining. The mill had shut down for the day. The world turned totally quiet. Not a soul was around us. Smoke from wood-stoves cooking dinner filled the cold air. The silence made me uneasy. I picked up a stick and tapped the hard ground.

Finally, Leroy cleared his throat. "Jolene, you know I like your momma."

I dug my heel into the red dirt.

"I like your momma *real* fine." He shook his head and laughed. "Oh, that woman can make me smile just by looking at me."

My stomach rolled and my forehead burned against the cool air.

"I guess what I'm trying to say is . . . I want to ask your momma to marry me."

My eyes stayed fixed on the ground, but I felt him staring at me.

"I'm hoping that will suit you just fine, too."

No, it won't suit me just fine, Mister. It never will suit me just fine. I didn't say anything though. I just kept scraping my heel into the dirt.

"I want to show something to you." He pulled a small box out of the sack and snapped it open. Inside was a plain, thin gold band. "It ain't nothing special, but it comes from my heart."

I stared at the ring, thankful that it didn't hold a shiny diamond. It was as plain as Leroy, but he looked at the band as if it did have a shiny diamond. And from the way he peered down at me, he must have wanted me to say I thought it was special, too.

"I have something else." His hand disappeared into the sack.

Here it is, I thought. *A bunch of peppermints to win me over. Only this time it won't work. Not this time. Not ever again.* But it wasn't peppermints that Leroy slid from the sack. It was the beautiful red velvet Momma had been aching for. "You know your momma loves red," he said, "and I think she'd be the prettiest thing wearing this. She'd look like a real ruby." He jabbed his elbow into my arm. "And don't be so gloomy. I bought you something, too."

This time, he pulled out the blue velvet. Just like Miz Logan's Valentine dress. I stared at the fabric, not knowing what to say.

Leroy placed the fabric on my lap. "I don't expect you to think of me as your daddy. Nobody can do that. Heck, I don't care if you call me Mister until the day I die. You can even put that over my grave. 'Here lies Mister.'" He chuckled and wiped his wet forehead with the handkerchief. If Leroy sweated like this in the winter, he must be like a soaked rag in the summer.

"I hope you'll warm up to the idea some. The velvet can be a gift from the two of us." He held out the velvet to me. "In fact, why don't you hide this some-

where in your house? We'll give it to your Momma the night I ask her to marry me."

I accepted the fabric just as the five o'clock train chugged down the tracks past us. *K-nook, k-nook, k-nook.* Usually I waved at the engineer in the front car and counted the beds of logs passing by. But I was too busy thinking about what Momma might say. She might not be impressed by the plain ring, but Momma was sure to tell Leroy yes after she saw that pretty velvet.

That evening, I thought about Leroy's proposal. That's why I squeezed between the wall and our bed with the fabric in one hand and Momma's scissors in the other. Then I cut the beautiful velvet into so many pieces it looked like a jigsaw puzzle.

CHAPTER 7

The next morning at recess, Florence and I played hopscotch. Before she took her turn, she asked, "Well?"

"Well what?" I asked back.

"What did Mr. Leroy Redfield want to tell you?" She looked like she was about to bust out of her blue coat from curiosity.

"Nothing."

"Is he going to ask your momma to marry him?"

"I said he didn't say nothing." Nothing I cared to remember. But I did remember what Leroy said, and worse—I remembered what I had done to that velvet.

Florence put her hands on her hips. "I can't believe you aren't going to tell me what he said. Not the way you tell everything."

"And I can't believe you're talking so much and asking such a nosy question. Just like a nosy old lady."

Florence hopped all the way to the number-ten square and whirled around. "Hmmph! I'll bet he's gonna ask your momma to marry him. You just don't want me to know."

The school bell rang before I had a chance to yank one of her braids.

At home, I hid the bag of velvet pieces under the bed, tucked inside a box of summer clothes. Friday night, Leroy picked Momma up for another dance. He wore a new white shirt and a black tie.

He kept shaking Grandpa's hand, saying, "How are you doing, Foster? Everything suiting you just fine? It sure is a nice evening." Finally, Grandpa had to yank his hand away.

When Momma walked into the room, Leroy pulled his handkerchief out and wiped his forehead. He guided Momma out of the house, winking at me before closing the door behind them.

I headed toward the drapes to take a peek, and frowned when Leroy bent to kiss Momma as he opened the truck door.

Grandpa said, "Let it be, child." I released the curtain and slid off the couch.

In bed, I tossed and turned. Shadows danced across the wall, and I wondered what Momma would say when Leroy showed her that plain ring. I knew Momma liked Leroy, but she wouldn't want to marry him. After all, she had Grandpa and me, and that was enough.

When I heard an owl hooting outside my window, I slipped out of my bed and looked between the curtains. About a million stars glittered in the clear sky. I wished I could find the Big Dipper. Maybe Daddy was looking down on me right now. I studied his picture, wishing I could remember his voice. But all I could remember was that whistle. Suddenly, I heard Leroy's old truck rattling down the street. When it stopped in front of our house, I jumped back into bed and pulled the sheets up to my chin.

They hadn't been gone more than an hour. Maybe Momma got mad at Leroy when he asked her to marry him. Maybe she said, "Leroy Redfield, of course I won't marry you. You better take me home right now."

But then I heard Leroy's heavy boots tromping across the floor along with Momma's light shuffle. Our bedroom door creaked open, and Momma whispered, "Jolene, are you asleep?"

"No, ma'am."

"Well, come on out here. We've got something to tell you and Grandpa."

I stumbled into the kitchen, which still smelled of the coffee Grandpa drank after dinner. I had to squint because the overhead light hurt my eyes. Next to the kitchen table, Leroy straddled a ladder-back chair, grinning from ear to ear. Grandpa leaned against the counter, rubbing his chin. His whiskers made a *whish-whish* sound.

Momma stood straight and proud. She held her left hand in front of me. The plain gold band circled her finger. My heart dropped into my stomach.

"Look, Jolene. Look what Leroy gave me. He's asked me to marry him. And I said yes." She gave Leroy a big kiss on the cheek. He tilted back his head and laughed.

Grandpa shook Leroy's hand. "Well, that's the finest news I've heard in a long time."

Leroy looked at me, but I didn't say a thing. This was the worst news I'd heard in my life. Everything would change now. Loud, stomping, talking Leroy would be around Momma always.

"Jolene," Leroy said. "Go get that other surprise." He winked at me.

My stomach churned, and my legs stayed stiff and refused to move.

"Another surprise?" Momma asked. "Leroy, you are going to spoil me rotten."

"That's the plan, woman. That's the plan." Leroy squeezed Momma's hand. He glanced back toward me and smiled. "Jolene, don't you remember where you hid the surprise?"

A shiver ran down my spine. I stared at the floor and said nothing.

"Jolene," Grandpa said, "go get the surprise Leroy's talking about."

I had no choice but to turn and head toward the room I shared with Momma. I thought about saying someone must have stole the fabric. Then I started to think about how Leroy would change everything in my family. After he married Momma, he would probably sleep in our room and I'd have to sleep on the couch. He would eat up our food. I'd be lucky if he left any crumbs for me. I wouldn't be able to hear the radio because of his booming voice. Momma would never go to the picture show with me again, because Leroy would be taking her dancing every Friday night. If Momma married loud, stomping, talking Leroy, everything would change.

By the time I reached under the bed, I was hopping mad. I threw the lid off the box and grabbed the sack. I marched back into the kitchen and handed it to Momma.

She was grinning as big as Leroy now. But when she reached into the sack and pulled out a handful of red and blue velvet pieces, her smile quickly shrank and her eyebrows shot up.

She glanced at Leroy. He had a look on his face like a whipped hound dog. He lowered his head and studied the floor. That must have been when she realized Leroy hadn't bought her a bag of scraps. She stared at me in a way that stung me like a dozen bumblebees.

Words flew from her mouth. "Jolene Jasmine Johnson, how could you?"

"Shame on you, child," Grandpa said.

Leroy touched Momma's arm. "Let her be, Ruby. It ain't the end of the world. It's just fabric."

"But, Leroy, the money it must have cost you." Momma glared at me like she was trying to read tiny words printed on the back of my eyeballs.

"It ain't the end of the world," Leroy repeated.

But I had a tightness crushing my heart, and it seemed like the end of the world to me.

CHAPTER 8

The next day, I had a sick feeling from my head to my toes. I had wanted to hurt Leroy by cutting up the fabric. I had wanted to keep Momma from marrying him. Instead, I had hurt Momma more than Leroy, and she was marrying him anyway. Whether I liked it or not.

I was thankful Grandpa worked Saturdays. He surely would have ordered me to read Bible verses all day about Cain, the Prodigal Son, and other misbehaving children.

Momma's silence was painful enough. Anytime the wood floor creaked or wind rattled the windows, the noise seemed as loud as a scream. But even worse, Momma wouldn't look at me.

Momma spent the morning ironing Miz Logan's Valentine dress. She pressed it from the inside out because heat would streak the fine fabric.

Whenever the iron cooled, I'd put it on the stove to reheat, then carry another hot one to Momma.

The sight of that pretty blue dress flowing over the ironing board like a waterfall gave me another pang of guilt. Now I'd never see how magnificent Momma and I would have looked in new velvet dresses.

If only I could make it up to Momma. But how? I couldn't glue fabric scraps together.

I had never seen Leroy get mad over anything, but I'd expected him to get mad about the velvet. He didn't. I wished he'd yelled and said he couldn't marry a woman with such a bad child. Then maybe I would feel better. But why should I care what he thought, anyway?

After lunch, Momma said, "I'm going to deliver Miz Logan's dress. I'll be back soon as I check the mail at the post office."

For the first time, she didn't ask if I wanted to go with her. And she knew how much I loved to go to Miz Logan's house and see her fine things. When the door clicked shut behind her, I felt so alone.

An hour later, Momma returned with an opened letter in one hand. She dragged her feet, and her forehead wrinkled like she was fretting over something. She dropped into Grandpa's chair and stared at the page.

"What's wrong, Momma?" I asked, hoping she noticed the broom in my hand.

"This letter is from Cousin Ophelia. She says Aunt Josephine is doing poorly." Aunt Josephine was Grandpa's sister who lived in New Orleans. "They don't expect her to live much longer." Momma's words sounded tiny, like raindrops falling in a fine mist.

"Poor Grandpa!" I said. "He'll be so sad. What are you going to do?"

"I don't know. I'll talk about it with Grandpa when he gets home." She stared out the window as if she expected to see him, but the sawmill was too far away.

Maybe we could visit Aunt Josephine in New Orleans. We could ride the bus or maybe the train. And I would finally see a big city. Bigger than nearby Alexandria, the only city I had ever visited. And best of all—Momma would get away from Leroy. Maybe she'd change her mind about marrying him.

Grandpa had told me about New Orleans more than once. He said people were scattered everywhere.

Street cars ran up and down tracks in the middle of the roads. The things he said he remembered most were the smells—spicy gumbos, French bread baking, and even garbage rotting on the streets.

Turning to me, Momma said, "Jolene, I forgot Miz Logan's scraps. I had so much spinning in my head today."

My gaze darted to the floor. I was probably the reason she had forgotten the scraps—me and the ruined velvet.

"You'll need to carry them back to her," she said. "Do it right now before you forget."

Harriet must have left for the day, because Miz Logan answered the door. Her red hair stuck up and out as if she hadn't combed it for a week. And she wore a pair of jeans like some of the men who worked at the mill. "Hello, Jo—lene, isn't it?"

"Yes, ma'am."

My mouth must have been hanging open, because she said, "Oh, don't mind me. I've been cleaning out the attic." I thought all Miz Logan did was have tea parties and fancy dances in her ballroom.

She smiled and accepted the sack of scraps. I wished I could have given our sack of scraps to her. As if giving the velvet away would make what I had done disappear.

She peeked inside the sack, then rolled down the edges, the paper crinkling. "Jolene, would you like to see what I do with these scraps?"

I nodded.

Opening the door wider, she motioned for me to step into the house. On the dining room table lay a beautiful quilt like I had never laid eyes on before. The only quilts I had seen looked like their names—Wedding Ring, Log Cabin, Sunbonnet Sue.

None of the pieces in Miz Logan's quilt matched. It wasn't finished yet, but it was already *magnificent*. I recognized fabric from her green dress and some ivory silk from an Easter dress Momma had made for her last spring. And there was the black taffeta from the New Year's ball dress, too. All stitched together with zigzag and flowery embroidery stitches.

"What do you think?" Miz Logan asked.

"I never saw such a pretty quilt." My hand started to reach toward it; then I remembered. Momma had warned me not to touch Miz Logan's things. I locked my hands together behind my back.

"It's called a crazy quilt. My grandmother had several in her home."

"Who's making it?" I asked.

"I am."

"*You* are?"

She chuckled. "Oh yes. Believe it or not. It's easy to

make. Kind of like sewing a jigsaw puzzle together. The more different shapes, the better."

I left Miz Logan's house with a smile on my face and a lift in my step. Rain started to pour from the sky, but I didn't care. I knew exactly how to make Momma feel better. I would sew a crazy quilt out of the crazy foolish thing I had done with that velvet.

Even though the rain soaked through my clothes, everything seemed brighter. Until I arrived home. Then Momma sat me down and said, "Your grandpa and I are going to New Orleans on Monday to visit Aunt Josephine."

The high hopes I had about seeing New Orleans sank to my toes. "But what about me?"

Momma looked me straight in the eye. "You can't miss school. Leroy says he will stay with you."

CHAPTER 9

Monday morning, Momma cooked a pot of red beans before she and Grandpa left for the bus heading toward New Orleans. I had mixed feelings about Momma leaving. After all, I wished I could go with her. And I sure didn't want to be alone with Leroy. Even though Harriet promised to look in on me, too. But it would give me a chance to work on the crazy quilt for Momma. Besides, I had two hours after school before Leroy would arrive.

That afternoon, I raced home with my lunch pail banging against my leg. I dashed into my bedroom and dug the scraps out of the sack.

Then I searched the house for scraps from the mill women's dresses to add to the velvet. Burgundy silk pieces poked out of books marking the last page I had read. Starched cotton remnants were tied around sticks, making aprons for my pretend dolls. I found a stack of calico squares, circles, and triangles Momma had cut when I was younger to teach me shapes. But even with the velvet, they didn't add up to enough scraps for a quilt.

I had no choice but to pull out the box of scraps I had been saving for Brenda Jane's dresses. Along with the mill women's scraps, there were the remnants from my three Easter dresses and the yellow cotton from the dress Momma made for my first day of second grade. There was a scrap from my Christmas dress. I had worn that dress only one time because I had spilled a glass of fruit punch on it. Momma had tried and tried to get the stain out, but couldn't.

Looking at those scraps on the floor was like looking through a photograph album of my life. I took a deep breath and arranged the pieces, trying to think of the best design for a quilt.

Soon, I heard Leroy's heavy steps on our porch. The front door creaked open. "Jolene?" he called in his booming voice.

I poked my head out of my bedroom door. "I'm in here, Mister."

He wore a silly grin like he had forgotten the hurt I caused him. He held a wind-up Victrola and a stack of records in his arms. His smile made me feel better until he said, "I just wanted you to know I was home. Do you mind if I play some music?"

"Suit yourself." I slammed the bedroom door. He was already calling our house "home." While I re-arranged quilt pieces, a trumpet played from the Victrola. Kitchen cabinets shut and squeaky drawers opened. I heard eggs cracking and a spoon sloshing in a bowl. Soon, the smell of red beans and something sweet baking drifted into my bedroom.

Half an hour later, Leroy clanked a spoon against a bowl and called out, "Supper time!"

Harriet knocked on the door and walked into our house with a basket. "Goodness almighty. I brought you some dinner, but it looks like you've got every-thing under control."

Not only Momma's red beans were on the table but also an iron skillet of yellow cornbread. Golden and crusty around the edges—the way I liked it best.

"That was right nice of you, Harriet," said Leroy. "Will it keep till tomorrow?"

"Sure will." Harriet set the basket down and walked

backward out of the house with a dazed look on her face. Before closing the door, she said, "Leroy, you are amazing."

Amazing didn't always mean good. My teacher said that skunks were amazing.

I sat down at the table. "Who made the cornbread?"

"I did," Leroy said. He looked as proud as Miz Myrtle did when she won a blue ribbon for her blackberry pie at the Fourth of July fair. "It was my momma's favorite recipe."

"Where is your momma?" I asked, hoping he might pay her a long visit and never return.

His smile disappeared. "She's dead. She died a long time ago." His voice sounded smaller than I'd ever heard it. Daddy's face flashed through my mind.

I decided to try Leroy's cornbread on account of his momma dying and since it was her favorite recipe. The slab of butter melted on the cornbread like a block of ice left in the hot sun. My mouth watered. The first bite I took was like eating heaven. Hog cracklings gave it a smoky flavor. I gobbled every crumb on my plate and tried not to glance at the remaining cornbread.

Leroy wrapped a dish towel around the hot skillet handle and lifted it to me. "Have another piece."

I pressed my lips together and shook my head.

He looked disappointed but kept holding the skillet in front of me. "It would please my momma's sweet soul to know you liked her cornbread enough to eat a second helping."

After what I had done to the velvet, I needed all the help in heaven I could get. I reached for another slice, this time saving some to sop up the red bean soup.

While we ate, happy brass sounds of a trumpet danced around us. "That's Louis Armstrong," said Leroy. "He's from New Orleans. He can play a trumpet like nobody's brother."

"New Orleans?"

"Uh-huh."

When the last song finished, the needle made a steady *thump, thump, thump.* Leroy jumped up and flipped the record over. "You'll like this song. It's called 'On the Sunny Side of the Street.'"

Thank goodness Momma kept a long cloth over the table so Leroy couldn't see my feet tapping to the music.

Later, Leroy washed the dishes, and I dried and put them away. I had hoped he would miss a spot so I could hand a dish back to him and point out his carelessness. But he cleaned those dishes and pots and pans so good they squeaked. He handed the last one to me and asked, "Want to listen to another record?"

"No sir, Mister. I got some work to do before I go to bed."

I marched away with my stomach stuffed with cornbread and beans, and my head racing with ideas for Momma's crazy quilt. I must have been crazy to take on such a big project.

CHAPTER 10

All week, I sewed those pieces of velvet together, wishing I could use Momma's Singer. As it was, I would be lucky to finish the quilt top in time. If I used Momma's sewing machine, I could finish the quilt top quicker and could start the quilting before she returned. But if I broke that old Singer, it wouldn't matter how pretty the quilt turned out. I'd be in trouble again.

Slowly, day by day, my crazy quilt grew. When it was big enough to cover half of our bed, I felt as proud as the day I received a perfect score on my math test.

At school Friday, we cut out hearts from pink and red paper because Valentine's Day was next week.

Then we taped them together and made a chain long enough to wrap around our room.

After school, Florence asked, "Where are you racing off to every day?"

"I can't tell you. Not yet, anyway." I dashed past her, my lunch pail smacking my leg. "See you tonight."

Florence didn't even wave. She just stood there with her blue mittens on her hips.

That evening, I bundled the quilt away before Florence's family picked up Leroy and me for the picture show. Leroy was so huge he had to sit in the back of the pickup with Florence and me. That night it was like Florence and I had traded places. I stayed quiet and she wouldn't shut up.

When I gazed up at the stars, Florence said, "Why don't you ask Mr. Leroy?"

I gave her a Hopalong Cassidy dirty-dog look like the one he gave the bad guys.

Leroy nudged his shoulder against mine. "Ask me what?"

Florence stared at me, waiting. When I didn't speak, she said, "Jolene wants to find the Big Dipper."

"No, I don't!" I snapped.

"Uh-huh!" she said. Wearing all that blue, Florence looked like a bossy old blue jay.

I expected Leroy to show off and point out the Big Dipper like he was some expert on the constellations.

Instead he leaned back against the pickup cabin. "If Jolene wants to know where the Big Dipper is, she can ask me herself."

He probably didn't know where the Big Dipper was, either.

Then he added, "And if she wants to know where the Little Dipper is, I'll be glad to show her that, too."

My eyes popped open. Our teacher hadn't told us anything about a *Little* Dipper.

Not another word was spoken until we reached Glenmora. I was missing Momma something fierce. Not even Hopalong Cassidy's name on the marquee lifted my spirits.

Leroy bought everyone's popcorn, even though Abe said, "You ought not do that."

In the balcony, Leroy sat right next to me. He breathed so loud, I thought he'd suck up all the air in the picture show. His big ol' chest rose up like a flat tire getting pumped. What if Momma came back from New Orleans and found out I had suffocated because Leroy—the man she was going to marry— didn't leave any air for her only daughter to breathe? I bet she wouldn't marry Leroy then.

I stopped listening to Leroy's breathing as soon as the movie began. Hopalong Cassidy's horse, Topper, was finer than Gene Autry's Champion. Topper was a magnificent white. He wore a black and silver saddle and bridle like the ones some horses wore in Glenmora's Fourth of July parade.

Everything we did that night made me miss Momma. We sat in the very same row Momma and I sat in last time. Only Leroy sat in Momma's seat. After the movie, we stood in line for an ice cream cone. I could almost hear Momma say, "Hurry up and choose, Jolene. Chocolate, vanilla, or strawberry?" And when Harriet wiped a drip of vanilla off Florence's chin, I felt like Topper had kicked me in the chest.

Just then, Leroy handed me a napkin and said, "Careful. You've got a streak of strawberry running down your face." I used the back of my hand instead.

On the ride back home, Florence asked, "Mr. Leroy, I'd sure like to know where that Big Dipper is."

I frowned at her, but she ignored me.

Leroy smiled and looked up, searching in the sky. A moment later, he pointed toward the northeast. "There he be. See those four bright stars?"

"Where?" asked Florence.

"Right there," he said. "That's the bowl. And see the handle? It's almost sticking straight up. Now looky over yonder. Just two stars to the west. That's the Little Dipper." He was talking to Florence, but he was looking at me.

CHAPTER 11

■ The next day, the sun warmed the cool air, making it feel more like a spring day. Harriet came over to pick up our laundry. Florence was with her, still wearing her blue coat.

"Ain't you hot, Florence?" Leroy asked.

"Yes sir."

Harriet walked by with a bundle of our clothes. "Florence catches a cold real easy."

Leroy rubbed his chin. "My momma, rest her soul, always said wearing too many clothes fetches a fever."

"See, Momma," said Florence. "Mr. Leroy's momma said I could fetch a fever."

One corner of Harriet's mouth turned up. "Well,

okay. You can switch your coat for a sweater when we get home."

Florence pranced toward the doorway, where I stood. "I like Mr. Leroy," she whispered to me before heading out the door.

That night Leroy knocked on my bedroom door. "Jolene, put on your Sunday church dress. I'm taking you out tonight."

"Where?" I asked.

"It's a surprise."

I didn't have time for surprises. Especially not from him. I wanted to finish the quilt top before Momma came back from New Orleans. At least the quilt top would show what the quilt would look like finished, even though it wouldn't be quilted yet. But I changed to my Sunday dress anyway.

Leroy looked like he did when he went on a date with Momma. He wore his white shirt and tie and smelled spicy like nutmeg.

"My, my," he said, his gaze fixed on me. "Don't you look fine."

Then his eyes rested on my dusty shoes, and he shook his head. "Oh, that won't do. No, that won't do at all." He pulled a handkerchief from his back pocket and knelt in front of me. Swishing the cloth back and forth, he gave my black patent Mary Janes a spit shine. He made me feel like a little kid. When he finished, I could see my face in the polished toes.

We rode in his truck out of mill town and past Barbers Creek. A distant light shone against the ebony sky. We seemed to be driving toward it. Even though the truck windows were rolled up, I heard music like the kind Duke Ellington and Count Basie played.

"Someone is sure playing their radio loud," I said.

Leroy smiled and kept driving toward the light. The closer we got, the louder the music became. The song was "Tunetown Shuffle." I had heard it a million times on the radio. A large, worn-down house came into focus. A sign hung out front read "Jimmy's Juke Joint." Cars and trucks parked outside while dozens of families poured into the house.

Leroy parked the truck on a grassy spot, and we joined the others inside. That's when I saw that the music wasn't coming from a radio but a real live band complete with a trumpet, guitar, and drums. One man playing a horn puffed out his cheeks while beads of sweat rolled down his face.

Women, men, and children danced to the jazz music. Everyone was dressed in their Sunday best. I was thankful for Leroy's spit shine.

The chain of red and pink paper hearts we made at school hung on the walls. I was in a dreamy daze when

Florence ran up to me. She wore her blue church dress and hair ribbons. "Hey, Jolene, did Leroy surprise you?"

"Uh-huh," I said, barely glancing at her. I was busy watching women and girls in bright swirling skirts like colorful toy tops spinning on the floor.

"They're dancing the jitterbug," said Florence. "Isn't this a great family Valentine dance?"

Only my family wasn't there. Just Leroy. I missed Momma and Grandpa something fierce. A haze of smoke from old men with pipes gathered in the corner. I felt a lonesome feeling sweep over me even though there were people laughing and dancing all around.

Suddenly, Leroy grabbed my hand, pulling me closer to the band. Before I had a chance to say anything, he swung me around as graceful as a man in a picture show. Leroy's feet moved to the song's beat. Like magic, mine did, too. I started laughing.

"You sound like your momma when you laugh," Leroy said. "You even look like her some."

"I do?"

"Yes sir-ree, you sure do."

When the song ended, another started. Leroy and I kept dancing. He spun me around and around. The times he had taken Momma dancing, I imagined him stepping on her skinny feet. But Leroy was such a

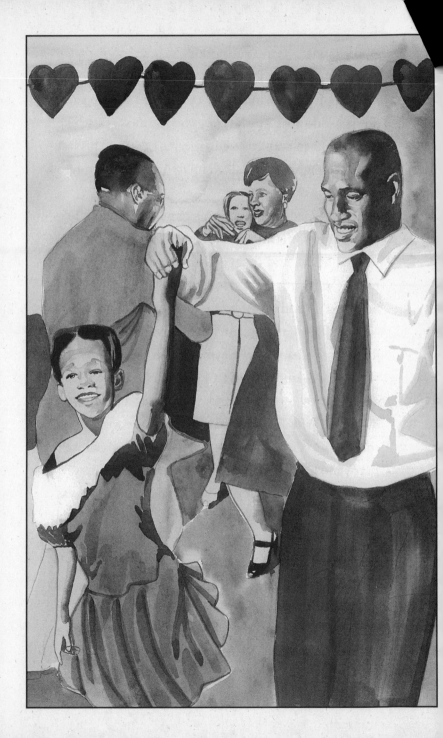

good dancer, he made me look like I could dance good, too. I guess he wasn't a clumsy ox, after all.

We didn't stop dancing except to eat a hot dog and drink a soda pop. The hot dogs had a smoky taste like they had been cooked over a fire. As Leroy ate his last bite, a young woman walked up to him and asked him to dance.

Leroy wiped his mouth on a napkin and said, "Beg your pardon, ma'am, but tonight I have a date." He winked at me and dragged me to the center of the room, and we started dancing again. That hot dog bounced up and down in my stomach.

Time flew fast like on Christmas Day. Before I knew it, the band was playing the last song. It was a slow song—kind of sad and soulful. I felt grown-up dancing with Leroy, his hand on my waist and mine on his upper arm. My other hand disappeared in his big rough one. Grandpa said a man earns his calluses. Leroy must work real hard cutting trees down.

I glanced around the room. Florence's daddy was spinning her. He looked at Florence like he was real proud of her. I looked up at Leroy and he was looking at me the same way.

"Jolene," he said, "I believe you inherited your momma's dancing feet."

My insides bubbled. Nothing pleased me more than knowing I could dance like Momma.

"In fact," Leroy said, "I think we're going to be known as the family with the dancing feet."

At the end of the song, we left the Juke Joint and headed toward the truck. It was strange. For the first time, I felt comfortable walking beside Mr. Leroy Redfield. Looking up in the dark sky, I saw the Big Dipper. And just like Leroy said, two stars over to the west was the Little Dipper.

Then Leroy did something that shook me to my core. Something I had never heard him do before. He whistled. He whistled a tune like the ones I remembered my daddy whistling years before. I slid my hand into his, and he suddenly stopped whistling. Car engines started and filled the night air like a band warming up before a show. Then Leroy tightened his grip around my hand and went back to whistling that song.

"Mister," I said.

"Yes, Jolene?"

"I'm sorry about cutting up that velvet."

CHAPTER 12

That weekend, I worked on the quilt. I worked twice as hard as before. Now I was sewing those stitches not only for Momma, I was sewing for Leroy, too.

At school Monday, I got so tired of Florence pestering me with her nosy questions. It was as if she was making up for all those times she didn't utter a peep.

"What kind of mischief are you up to?" she asked as if she were a grown-up. I think I liked her better when she didn't have much to say.

"Okay, I'll show you after school. But you have to promise to keep it a secret."

On the way home, I told her what I had done with the velvet.

Her eyes grew as big as giant marbles. "You didn't!" she said.

Then I proudly pulled out the quilt top. It was almost finished. She looked at it real hard, curled her lips, and raised her eyebrows. Finally, she said, "I think I'd like it better all in one piece. That way you could have had a velvet dress."

I frowned. "I know that, silly, but I can't turn back now. What's done is done."

"And you sure done it!" she exclaimed with her hands on her hips and her head darting from side to side. She reminded me of a hen prancing around a chicken yard.

I wished I hadn't told her. The way she looked at the quilt top made me think it was a dumb idea. And she was right, it wasn't as pretty as it was in one piece.

Her hand reached out and brushed over the velvet pieces.

"Uh-uh!" I lifted her hand away from the quilt. "You'll wear the sheen off."

Florence shrugged her shoulders. "What are you going to sign on it?"

"What do you mean?"

"My grandmother signs her quilts in the corner.

That way the people she gives them to will know they are special."

"I'll have to think about that."

"Well, I have to go home." She stood up and started out the door, then whipped around. "I like your quilt," she said. "I bet your momma will like it."

And Leroy, too, I hoped.

Later that week, Momma and Grandpa returned from New Orleans. Momma filled our house with her rose scent. I had been lonesome for that smell and hadn't even known it.

"Reach in my pocket," Grandpa said.

My hand pulled out golden round candy wrapped in thin paper. "Pralines! Thank you, Grandpa!"

He nodded and sank into his chair. Even though he was near, he seemed far away.

"How's Aunt Josephine?" I asked.

Momma stroked the top of my head. "She died, honey. That's why it took us so long. We stayed for the funeral."

Leroy touched Momma's arm. "Sit down, Ruby. I'll make us some supper."

"You cook?" Momma asked.

"Oh yes, ma'am," I said. "Leroy can cook. Will you make some of your momma's cornbread?"

Leroy chuckled. "It would be my pleasure."

"Can we put on the Louis Armstrong record?" I

turned to Momma. "He can play like nobody's brother."

Momma plopped onto the couch. "Well, it looks like a lot happened while we were away."

Leroy did a quick shuffle with his feet. "Oh, it did, Ruby-Gal. It sure 'nuff did."

Grandpa kept quiet. I guess he was thinking about his sister.

"Prop up your leg, Grandpa," I said. "I'll heat your hot water bottle."

Grandpa smiled. "A lot *sure* did happen while we were gone."

The morning of the wedding, it rained. But by the time one o'clock arrived, the clouds rolled away and sunshine poured from the sky.

"It's a perfect day," Leroy said. "A perfect day to be married."

Aunt Josephine must have thought a lot of Momma because she left Momma her white lacy wedding dress. Momma looked beautiful. I felt pretty, too, wearing last year's pink Easter outfit. Even Leroy looked handsome. Kind of.

After the preacher pronounced them husband and wife, Momma and Leroy jumped over a broom. Just like Grandpa's parents did when they married in the slave days.

Momma and Leroy cut the butter cream cake, and I served a slice to each guest.

After they opened their presents, I said, "There's one more. It's from me."

Momma glanced at Leroy, but he shrugged his shoulders.

My hands shook as I handed them the box with my quilt top inside. Maybe it was a dumb idea. Momma and Leroy probably wanted to forget about that velvet. And besides, it wasn't even quilted yet.

Momma opened the box, lifted the quilt top, and smiled. First it was a small smile. Then it grew real big—big as the Mississippi River. Red and blue velvet mixed together with the pieces of burgundy silk and calico. For a moment, I swear it looked more magnificent than Miz Logan's quilt.

"Jolene!" Momma shook her head back and forth. She pointed to a patch in the quilt. "There's your school dress. And your Easter dresses!" Her eyes grew misty. "It's beautiful, honey. When did you find time to do this?"

"While you were in New Orleans. Read the corner."

She pulled the corner up close to her face and read aloud.

" 'To Momma and Leroy on their Wedding Day, February 24, 1940, With love, Jolene.' "

Momma hugged me. "Thank you, Jolene."

MOMMA AND LEROY ON THEIR
WEDDING DAY
FEBRUARY 24, 1940

Even Grandpa smiled and said, "Well, I'll be.

But Leroy didn't say a word. I wondered if he was finally mad at me for what I had done to the velvet. Maybe he was thinking about how much prettier it would have been made into fine dresses.

I held my breath, waiting. Waiting for him to do something. Anything. Then I saw a tear glisten in the corner of his eye. I thought he'd yank out his handkerchief and wipe it away, but he let it roll down his cheek. He squeezed Momma and rocked her back and forth. Back and forth like Grandma's old rocker. Then he stretched out an arm and motioned for me to join them. I felt the air fill my lungs again as I stepped under his arm. Grandpa stood nearby, smiling at the three of us.

"Come here, Daddy," Momma said, motioning Grandpa to us.

He came over and slid in between Momma and me, closing our family circle. Our family with the dancing feet—Grandpa, Momma, Leroy, and me. And that's enough.